Frog Freak Out!

Ali Sparkes

illustrated by
Ross Collins

OXFORD
UNIVERSITY PRESS

OXFORD

UNIVERSITY PRESS

Great Clarendon Street, Oxford OX2 6DP

Oxford University Press is a department of the University of Oxford.
It furthers the University's objective of excellence in research, scholarship,
and education by publishing worldwide in

Oxford New York

Auckland Cape Town Dar es Salaam Hong Kong Karachi
Kuala Lumpur Madrid Melbourne Mexico City Nairobi
New Delhi Shanghai Taipei Toronto

With offices in

Argentina Austria Brazil Chile Czech Republic France Greece
Guatemala Hungary Italy Japan Poland Portugal Singapore
South Korea Switzerland Thailand Turkey Ukraine Vietnam

Oxford is a registered trade mark of Oxford University Press
in the UK and in certain other countries

Text © Ali Sparkes 2011
Illustrations © Ross Collins 2011
SWITCH logo designed by Dynamo Ltd

The moral rights of the author have been asserted

Database right Oxford University Press (maker)

First published 2011

British Library Cataloguing in Publication Data
Data available

ISBN: 978-0-19-273244-6
1 3 5 7 9 10 8 6 4 2

Printed in Great Britain

Paper used in the production of this book is a natural,
recyclable product made from wood grown in sustainable forests.
The manufacturing process conforms to the environmental
regulations of the country of origin.

With grateful thanks to John Buckley, fabulous amphibian* and reptile guru, and ARC, without whom this book might be full of embarrassing errors.

For Maisy, Lewis and Rosie

(*And no, I don't mean John Buckley is a fabulous amphibian)

Danny and Josh
and Charlie

Josh and Danny might be twins but they're NOT the same!
Josh loves newts, frogs and toads. Danny can't stand
them and would much prefer to be abseiling than admiring
amphibians. Their new friend, Charlie, thinks frogs are
AWESOME but will she feel the same once she's been
SWITCHed into one?

Danny

- FULL NAME: Danny Phillips
- AGE: 8 years
- HEIGHT: Taller than Josh
- FAVOURITE THING: Skateboarding
- WORST THING: Creepy-crawlies and tidying
- AMBITION: To be a stunt man

Josh

- FULL NAME: Josh Phillips
- AGE: 8 years
- HEIGHT: Taller than Danny
- FAVOURITE THING: Collecting insects
- WORST THING: Skateboarding
- AMBITION: To be an entomologist

Charlie

- FULL NAME: Charlie Isobel Wexford
- AGE: 8
- HEIGHT: Perfect
- FAVOURITE THING: Bungee jumping
- WORST THING: Sitting still
- AMBITION: To eat mint choc chip ice cream in space

CONTENTS

Soggy Horror

'It's raining sideways,' said Danny. 'In fact, I'm fairly sure it's just started raining *up*.' He slammed the cabin door behind him and thumped down heavily on the bed next to Josh.

'It'll probably stop soon,' sighed Josh, who was peering at a book in the dim light. The energy-saving bulbs in the cabin were orangey and not very bright.

'You said that yesterday,' grumbled Danny. 'And the day before.'

'Well, I'm not a weather forecaster!' said Josh. 'I don't know! I'm just trying to be cheerful.'

'Just trying to be cheerful,' mimicked Danny in a silly high voice. He kicked a bucket which was collecting some drips from the ceiling. 'Why did I ever say yes to this stupid summer camp?'

'It was the abseiling,' said Josh, still reading. 'And the canoeing. And the den building and the tree climbing.'

Danny folded his arms and huffed. There had been *some* fun—bits of it—in between the rain. The abseil was great; even Josh had had a go although he'd looked as white as a sheet in his ropes and safety helmet as he stepped off the ten metre high platform. The canoeing had been good too. But both these things had been cut short when the rain and wind got so bad the instructors couldn't actually *see* the kids any more.

Since then there had been indoor stuff going on. To start with, loads of them had been playing handheld computer games for a few hours in the big canvas tepee, and that was a brilliant laugh . . . right up until Sergeant Major had stomped in and confiscated them all.

'Didn't you read the rules?' he bellowed as the rain drummed loudly above them. 'Nobody should have brought any computer games or mobile phones or gadgets with them! This is Outdoor Action Camp—not Suction Your Eyeballs

To A Beeping Screen Camp. Here—read some pamphlets on how to light a campfire instead.'

His name was Steve, but every kid there called him Sergeant Major because he was so shouty. There was a rumour that he'd been a prison guard in his last job. He had a jaw like a breezeblock and tiny dark eyes that glittered malevolently at any kid who didn't instantly do as they were told. Several had been refused puddings and treats by Steve for misbehaving (Danny on day one!) and the man shouted so loudly whenever he was angry that the rooks in a nearby clump of trees would scatter into the sky, cawing with terror.

'Ooooooh! LOOK!' Josh suddenly threw down his book and shot across the floor of the cabin to scoop something up in his hands.

'Whaaa-aat?' asked Danny, anxiously, and Callum and Sayid sat up on their bunks to see what was going on.

'What a beauty!' murmured Josh, staring into his cupped palms.

Danny stepped back a bit. He knew where this was going. 'What have you got now, you freaky little bug boffin?' he asked.

'A nursery web spider!' said Josh and opened out his palms gleefully. A large yellowy-brown spider sat there, its front four legs clumped together in pairs so it looked as if it might have only six. Its abdomen was long and pointed. It started to scuttle up Josh's arm.

'Eeeeeeeugh!' Danny shuddered. He hated creepy-crawlies. Even though he'd been one—quite a few times.

'Ah come on—she's gorgeous,' said Josh, and Sayid came to have a look, squinting through his spectacles. So did Callum, although he kept his distance and held his Marvel comic annual across his chest.

'Gorgeous?' Danny stared at his brother. Sometimes he had difficulty believing that they really were related—but being identical twins proved they must be. 'Josh . . . you need to get out more!'

Sayid and Callum soon lost interest and
wandered out of the cabin, holding their raincoats
over their heads, to see what was for lunch.

'I'm amazed you're still such a baby about
these things,' said Josh as the nursery web spider
reached his shoulder. 'You've *been* one!'

'Yes . . . and I've also nearly been eaten alive by
one too, remember?'

Josh had to admit this was true. Over the last
few weeks he and his brother had been turned

into spiders, flies, grasshoppers, ants, daddy-long-legs and even great diving beetles. And nearly every time something had tried to eat them. While Danny was a fly he'd been captured by a female spider and wrapped up in silk—a tasty snack for later on. He was half a second away from being injected with gut-pulverizing venom when he was rescued.

'I wouldn't mind being SWITCH sprayed and turned into one of these, though, for just a few minutes,' said Josh. 'They're amazing hunters. They don't use webs—they just hide under a leaf and POUNCE!' He shook his spidery shoulder at Danny and Danny squeaked and jumped back. He might be super brave while dangling over the edge of a high building on a rope or turning upside down through the water in a canoe . . . but he just couldn't STAND creepy-crawlies.

'I thought you said you NEVER wanted to be SWITCHed again,' said Danny. 'You said you never even wanted to SEE Petty Potts over the fence. Mum thought you were really rude when you ignored Petty in the Post Office last week.'

'Yeah, well,' said Josh, gently putting the spider back down into the corner where it vanished into a crack in the floorboards. 'Mum doesn't know that our sweet old neighbour is actually a mad genius scientist who's turned us into creepy-crawlies with her SWITCH spray quite a few times now.'

'True,' agreed Danny. 'She'd probably have her arrested if she did.'

'Still . . . ' said Josh, ' . . . at least we're safe from Petty Potts and her sneaky experiments. We're miles away in the middle of nowhere.'

'Yep.' Danny grinned. 'No chance of that mad granny catching up with us here! Shall we go and find out what's for lunch then?'

'OK,' said Josh. They grabbed their waterproofs and opened the door.

And SCREAMED.

Standing in the dripping doorway of the log cabin was Petty Potts.

Petty, Charlie—Charlie, Petty

'AAAAAARGH!' screamed Josh. And Danny agreed.

'Pleased to see me?' Petty Potts beamed. Her grey hair was covered with a waxed cotton beanie hat and her glasses were steamed up. Her shiny red waterproof coat glistened eerily in the orangey light and she smelt worryingly of chemicals, like a school science lab.

'What are YOU doing here?' squawked Josh.

'I was going to ask you the same thing!' said Petty.

'We're at summer camp!' said Danny. 'But shouldn't you be doing something sinister in your secret dungeon—like SWITCHing some defenceless pigeon into a woodlouse or something?'

'It's not a dungeon!' Petty bristled (literally—the whiskers on her chin stood up). 'It's a state-of-the-art laboratory, cunningly hidden under my garden, where I perform my acts of genius. I DO wish you wouldn't be so melodramatic, Danny.'

'So—why are you here?' Josh eyed her suspiciously. Even though Petty had saved their lives once or twice, neither of them trusted her as far as they could throw her (and that would not be far). Petty was just too swept up with BUGSWITCH and REPTOSWITCH experiments to give two hoots about their safety.

'I am a camp counsellor!' She grinned. 'I am here to look after all you small children . . . as if I were your loving auntie. Isn't that nice?'

Josh pulled Petty into the cabin and shut the door behind her. 'Petty—you are NOT planning to SWITCH any of the kids here, are you?' he demanded, really alarmed now.

'Of course not,' said Petty. 'As IF! No . . . I really wanted to get away for a while and just relax and share the company of happy young minds . . . that's all.'

'So,' Danny eyed her suspiciously, 'nothing at all to do with your Serum Which Instigates Total Cellular Hijack?'

'Not at all,' said Petty, grinning again. 'I'm on holiday too. I don't plan to hijack the cells of anyone or instigate anything this week. Although you might like to know that the REPTOSWITCH formula is very nearly complete.'

'How can you complete it?' asked Josh. 'You never found the final crystal cube with the last bit of the secret formula!'

He and Danny exchanged uneasy glances. They had been helping Petty find the REPTOSWITCH formula all summer. It was hidden in six parts, each part in code in a crystal cube. They'd found them all—but the very last one was not in Petty's lab. Right at this moment it was in a thick old sock at the bottom of Danny's camp holdall. They'd decided Petty was too dangerous to have it when she nearly killed an old enemy a couple of weeks ago after SWITCHing him into a cockroach.

'Well, I'm hoping I can somehow work out the missing bit,' went on Petty. 'And in the meantime, as a side experiment I've also concocted AMPHISWITCH!'

'AMPHISWITCH?' Josh couldn't help the tiniest flutter of excitement. He had always adored amphibians.

'Yes! Reptiles and amphibians are quite similar, you see . . . and although the missing part of the REPTOSWITCH formula is flummoxing me when it comes to perfecting reptile SWITCHing, the parts I have got were nine tenths of what I needed for amphibians. I put my brilliant mind to work on some calculations which are far too complicated for you to understand . . . and discovered the final bit for AMPHISWITCH last week! Now I can SWITCH you into a frog or a toad or a newt!' Petty's eyes gleamed through the condensation on her glasses.

Danny and Josh gave her a stony look.

'But not NOW, obviously,' simpered Petty. 'We're all on holiday. No SWITCHing, no experiments . . . just lots of jolly FUN! So—what do you say? Shall we go and get lunch? It's cottage pie and peas . . . my favourite!'

'OK,' said Josh, and Danny nodded. They followed Petty out into the rain, which really did seem to be going up as well as sideways, and made for the canteen cabin.

Petty smiled happily at them as they stepped outside into a big wet gust of wind, but Josh and Danny didn't smile back. They didn't look at her at all. So they didn't see the four plastic spray bottles hidden in her coat as the gust blew it open.

Charlie was doing a handstand on a dining table when they walked into the canteen cabin. A dozen or so kids were counting and clapping. It seemed she'd been handstanding for quite some time, because they were up to sixty-six.

'Keep counting,' squeaked Charlie, her face beetroot red and her many beaded black plaits dangling between her elbows. She was wearing the Outdoor Action Camp uniform of blue shorts and a lurid orange T-shirt (the instructors and camp counsellors liked to see them easily at a distance) but even upside down Danny could see that she'd 'improved' her T-shirt with a black marker pen. The big smiley on it now had fangs, dripping blood.

'Good lord,' said Petty. 'Does she do this sort of thing often?'

'All the time,' Danny grinned. 'That's Charlie Wexford.' He thought Charlie was brilliant. In the three days since they'd arrived Charlie had been the most punished kid on site. She'd climbed up on the girls' dormitory cabin roof and yodelled (no pudding), canoed off on her own down the river and got herself happily lost for an hour (no pudding twice and a big Sergeant Major shouting session), cut a girl's hair with 'borrowed' kitchen scissors (all her sweets confiscated and Sergeant Major shouting for nearly half an hour)—and made up alternative words for the Outdoor Action Camp campfire song.

The proper campfire song went:

We love to swim, we love to climb,
We love to cook outdoors and sing,
We love to build a campfire
And be jolly about everything!

Charlie's version went:

We love to play computer games,
We love to watch TV and snack,
We hate this mouldy weather
And we all want to go back.

After the handheld computer games were confiscated everyone learned Charlie's version with gusto. Sergeant Major had ROARED at them for nearly an hour around that campfire . . . And Charlie was sent to bed without supper.

But nothing seemed to put her off.

Seventy-five, seventy-six, seventy-seven . . .

'Dear child, your head is going to pop,' observed Petty Potts, peering at Charlie curiously. Charlie's face was purple now.

'I feel fine,' gurgled Charlie.

'Well that's perfectly all right then,' said Petty, taking a seat at the table and beaming closely at Charlie's upended face. 'As long as you don't mind your blood pooling in your skull, leading to congestion, vessel rupture, seizures and possibly death. So, everyone . . . when do we get lunch?'

Charlie looked a little worried and her legs wobbled. Then she crashed down right into the cutlery and salt and pepper tray EXACTLY as the door flew open and Sergeant Major strode in.

'WEXFOOOOOOORD!' bellowed Sergeant Major and everyone scattered away from the table in horror. Now they would ALL miss pudding.

'Hello, Steve,' said Petty, getting to her feet and offering the camp leader a sickly smile. 'Don't mind little Charlie here. I asked her to assist me with an experiment on the pressure of blood on the inverted brain.'

'Wuff-uff-uff!' spluttered Sergeant Major. His mouth had been open and he'd been taking in a big lungful of air, ready to shout so loudly that everyone would be pasted against the far wall. The new camp counsellor lady had taken the wind out of him . . . literally.

'You remember I told you I'm a scientist,' explained Petty, taking off her hat. 'So when children ask questions I do like to explain things thoroughly to them. That's why this sweet young lady was performing a handstand. But I can see that we've been a little over enthusiastic. Don't worry about it at all, Steve. We'll soon have the knives and forks shipshape. Shut your mouth now, there's a dear.' And she actually leaned over and pushed Sergeant Major's chin up until his mouth snapped shut with a clunk of teeth. He looked absolutely astonished.

'What's your name?' asked Charlie when they were all sitting down to cottage pie and peas a few minutes later.

'Miss Potts,' said Petty. 'I've taken over from Miss Chatham, who, as you probably know, came out in a nasty rash of boils yesterday.'

'Well, Miss Potts,' grinned Charlie, waving a fork of mashed potato towards her and narrowing her dark brown eyes.

'You are COOL!'

Josh and Danny, sitting on either side of the cool Miss Potts, shook their heads and groaned.

'Thank you, dear,' Petty replied. 'Call me Petty.'

'We're watching you!' warned Danny in a low voice, leaning towards her. 'Don't you try SWITCHing Charlie!'

'Danny, when will you learn to trust me?' sighed Petty with a look of great sorrow, thinking of the hidden SWITCH spray bottles inside her coat. 'You're all quite safe with me . . .'

Moonlit Misadventure

Charlie's most daring feat took place that night. At around 2.30 a.m. there came a series of small sharp knocks on their door. It sounded like a squirrel with urgent news.

Danny blearily slid out of his top bunk, narrowly avoiding standing on Josh's head below, and went to the door. Outside it had stopped raining and there in the dim light of the moon stood Charlie in her pyjamas, clutching several shiny rectangle things.

'My DS! WHOA!' yelled Danny, scooping up his computer gadget in delight.

'Shhhhh!' Charlie looked around edgily. 'Don't wake everyone up, you plopstick!' She stepped inside and pushed the door shut with her shoulder, grinning wickedly. 'I couldn't sleep,

I was sooooo bored. So I thought I'd get these back for us.'

Callum and Sayid were now awake. They got out of their bunks and seized their own gadgets, whooping with joy. Josh sat up in bed, smiling and shaking his head. He hadn't brought a computer game with him—creepy-crawlies were his kind of fun. 'You're going to get into SUCH trouble this time, Charlie,' he said. 'How did you do it?'

'I noticed where Sergeant Major left the key to the confiscation cupboard while I was in the camp office getting shouted at for the hair thing,' said Charlie with a casual shrug. 'It's on a hook right next to his bunk in the room next door.' She held up the key, an old-fashioned iron one with a fob hanging off it—one of those soft plastic bulb-like fobs with a mini yellow fish floating in red water inside it.

'I still can't believe you cut Sally's hair,' guffawed Callum.

'She wanted me to! I didn't make her!' said Charlie, dropping the key back in her pyjama top pocket. 'Why all the fuss?'

They settled on to the bunks and switched on the gadgets with assorted jingly noises and flashes of colour. The power chargers were still in their drawers so they hooked up to the mains and went on gaming for hours. Josh joined in a bit, although mostly he watched. Until he noticed something slightly worrying.

'Erm . . . guys,' he said, peering out of the window. 'The sun is nearly up. Don't you think we ought to get some sleep now?'

'Sheeesh!' Charlie stood up, looking worried.'I'd better get these back in the cupboard and the key back on the hook before Sergeant Major wakes up.'

'It's only 5.15,' said Sayid, looking at his watch.

'But he gets up early to go running,' said Charlie. 'His cabin's next to ours and I hear his alarm clock go off at six o'clock, every morning, and then he hoofs past our window ten minutes later.'

'We'll come with you,' offered Josh, clapping Danny's shoulder. 'We can keep watch while you go in.' Sayid and Callum handed back their switched off games and scrambled back into their bunks.

It was cool and fresh as they stepped out into the dawn and made their way quietly across towards the cabin which housed the office and Sergeant Major's room at the far end of the camp. As they passed the large pond Josh paused, entranced by a chorus of purring croaks. 'Listen! It's the frogs! The froggy dawn chorus is just starting!' His eyes were shining.

'We haven't got time,' hissed Danny, feeling very nervous now that the sun was so far up. He didn't fancy meeting up with Sergeant Major while clutching all these gadgets.

'No—I want to see!' whispered Charlie and ran after Josh who was now kneeling at the edge of the pond, pointing to the little greeny-brown noses and pop-up eyes of six or seven frogs in the dark water.

Charlie dropped the games on the bank and leaned in to look. 'Ooooh—they're so sweet, aren't they? Ooh—look—did you see that one go? He just hopped right out from under that rock and into the water!'

'More "leapt" than hopped, really,' said Josh. 'Toads hop, frogs leap. Actually, toads aren't even

that good at hopping . . . they mostly crawl about.
They're not half as energetic as frogs. They're dead
easy to catch.'

'Oh here we go,' muttered Danny. 'Boffin attack.
Come ON, you two!'

'Wait! I want to see another frog leap!' said
Charlie, crouching next to Josh. She anchored her
hands on the bank and leant right out across the
water, fascinated. There was a plop. But it wasn't a
frog. It was the key to the confiscation cupboard.

Josh and Charlie squeaked in horror and tried
to grab it as it sank through the water, but it was
gone in a second, lost in the dark depths.

'Noooo!' gasped Charlie and shoved her arm in after it, scrabbling around frantically. Josh joined her but all they succeeded in doing was stirring up all the silt and weed, making it impossible to see a thing. They couldn't feel anything key-like—just the rather slippery gooeyness of waterweed, algae and the odd squirm of something living.

Eventually, as Danny looked on in horror, they slumped down on the bank and stared at each other, aghast. 'We're done for,' said Josh. 'We can't get the games back in the cupboard or the key back on the hook. And Sergeant Major could wake up at any minute!'

Charlie sighed and shook her head. 'No . . . you're not done for. It was me who did it . . . me who lost the key . . . you two go back to bed and I'll own up.'

'But you'll be sent home!' said Danny. 'That's what they said after the hair thing. One more strike and you're out!'

'Ah well,' shrugged Charlie. 'It's been fun. But unless one of us turns into a frog and goes diving for the key, that's that. I'll be OK. Mum was hoping I'd last the full ten days . . . ' She bit her lip. ' . . . but I'm always disappointing her, so it won't be a surprise. Why are you two looking all funny?'

Josh was staring at Danny and Danny was staring right back and now he started shaking his head. 'You've got to be kidding!' he said. 'You have GOT to be kidding!'

Josh looked at his watch. 'We've got half an hour if we're lucky,' he said.

'What are you two on about?' said Charlie, peeling some pondweed off her arm.

'Erm . . . we might be able to help,' said Josh, detaching a water snail from his wrist.

'Josh! NO!' hissed Danny. 'You can't!'

'Look—she's not just any girl,' said Josh. 'She'll handle it!'

'Handle what?' said Charlie, looking very puzzled.

'Charlie—you said one of us needed to turn into a frog,' said Josh. 'Well . . . one of us can.'

'OK,' said Charlie. 'If you say so.'

'I'm going to tell her,' Josh said to Danny, who slapped his hand across his eyes and groaned. 'Listen, Charlie—don't interrupt, there's no time. We CAN turn into frogs—and we're going to do it just as soon as we've woken Petty Potts up.'

Hop Till You Plop

'Which one of you is SWITCHing?' Petty eyed all three of them eagerly as they stood beside the pond. She was also wearing pyjamas (thick tartan ones) with wellingtons and her dark red raincoat which she now opened out, revealing the four SWITCH spray bottles held in its lining. 'Frog, toad or newt?' she added, like a mad waiter presenting a menu.

'Frog! Frog!' Charlie jumped up and down in immense excitement, clapping her hands. 'Oh, I can't believe this! It's so amazing!'

'Wait—you're not going!' said Josh. 'I am! It's far too dangerous for a g—for a beginner.'

Charlie narrowed her eyes at him. 'You meant "for a girl"! That's what you were going to say, wasn't it?'

45

'No—yes—look, it doesn't matter!' spluttered Josh. 'It was my plan and believe me, you have no idea how terrifying it is to be SWITCHed. Everything wants to eat you!'

'You've done it loads of times!' pointed out Charlie. 'So it can't be that bad.'

'Yes, but only because Petty tricked us into it! Mostly, anyway . . .'

'Excuse me! The genius scientist is actually PRESENT, you know!' interrupted Petty. 'And pardon me, but didn't you ASK for my help this time?'

'Sorry, Petty . . . but you know what I mean,' said Josh.

'Yes . . . you're never all that worried about how chewed we might get, are you?' added Danny, giving her a glare.

'Nonsense. I am always filled with great concern for you,' scoffed Petty. 'Now—who's first?'

'Me! Me!' Charlie started jumping again, as if she was practising. 'Frog! I want to be a frog. Spray me!'

'Charlie—I said—' began Josh.

'Don't care!' said Charlie. 'SWITCH me, Petty, or I'll tell everyone your secret. Turn me into a frog and I will NEVER breathe a word.'

Petty was taking no chances. She pulled out a bottle with 'A1' written on it in marker pen, and sprayed it at Charlie's head. There was just time for a thrilled squeak before Charlie vanished and a frog sat at their feet, grinning in a very delighted way.

'Petty! SWITCH me NOW!' commanded Josh. 'You shouldn't have let her go first! If she gets eaten I will NEVER forgive you!'

Three seconds later there were two frogs on the bank. Petty waved the bottle at Danny and wiggled her eyebrows. He sighed. 'Ah, go on then . . .'

And then there were three.

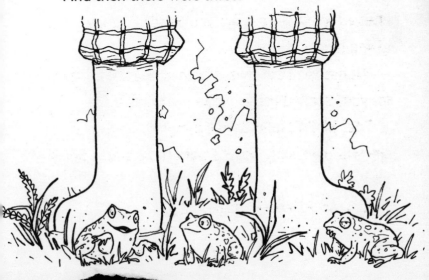

Pond Life

'Ribbet! Ribbet! Ribbet!' yelled Charlie, leaping up and down like a bug-eyed ballerina. 'WOW! Ribbet! Ribbet!'

'Why do you keep going ribbet?' said Josh, extending his impressive back legs and peering down the length of them.

'I'm speaking frog!' Charlie giggled.

'Right—if you say so,' said Josh. 'But actually, common British frogs don't go ribbet. We're speaking froggish now but the only frog which actually goes "ribbet" is the kind in Disney movies. An American one.'

PLOP! Charlie landed with a squelch, right in front of Josh. 'Well I like ribbetting! Will other frogs understand us?' she asked, her bulbous eyes shining with delight. They were yellowy-gold around the outer edges with large oval black pupils in the centre.

'Yes, probably,' chuckled Josh. He was pretty thrilled to be a frog too. 'They might freak out when they see us, though. We might still smell a bit human. They might scream. They don't ribbet but they can scream.'

Danny was ready to scream at any moment. 'What's going to eat me this time, Josh?' he queried, looking around edgily. Behind him the titanic shape of Petty Potts was standing very still. Her foot, in its rubber boot, was the size of a car.

'Ummm . . . big birds might try,' said Josh.
'Mammals, too. Snakes. A fox would make a quick
snack of you, no problem. A cat too, maybe,
although mostly they just like to play.'

Danny shuddered, the ripples of horror visible
across his mottled throat. So did Josh. He'd been
'played with' by a cat before, on the day they were
SWITCHed into grasshoppers. 'Let's go!' he said,
and leapt into the water.

Two more sploshes and plumes of bubbles
followed him in and at once the world was utterly
different. They were floating through a dim watery
universe, filled with elegantly wafting weed,
spinning particles of silt, tumbling black water
snails and darting brown fish.

'Wooooooooooow!' marvelled Charlie. 'Look at meeeeee!' Keeping her arms close to her body, she kicked her long legs and webbed feet and shot through the water at speed. Josh copied her and caught up in two seconds. 'How come I can talk under water?' asked Charlie. 'I'm not opening my mouth!'

'You're sending vibrations,' explained Josh, using his own vibrations. 'Through your throat muscles and skin. Clever, isn't it?'

'Wait for me!' called Danny and followed close behind. 'Josh! Wait! Is there anything down here which will eat me?'

Josh turned in the water and watched his brother approaching. Danny looked truly elegant. Josh had always loved frogs. Lots of people thought they were slimy and revolting but Josh saw only their sleek shiny beauty as they swam and their amazing leaping ability on dry land; their clever pulsating throats pushing air deep down into their bodies and their amazing skin, able to adapt to water or dry land.

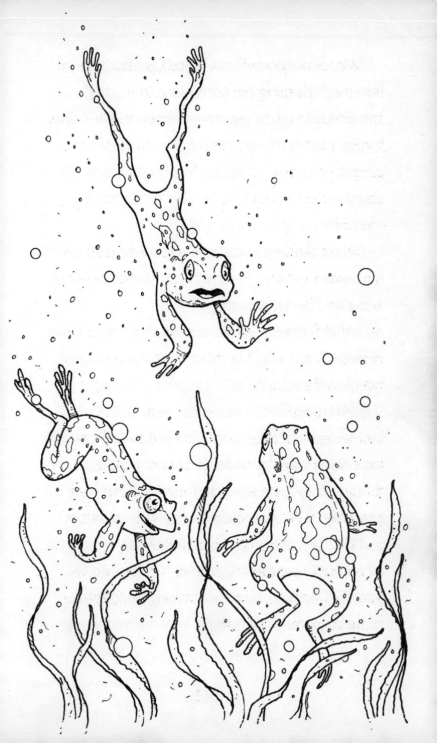

'We're OK down here!' he called. 'There's nothing big enough to go for us in the pond. Another frog might jump on your back in springtime but not in summer. I can't see any around now, anyway. Ooooh this is SOOOO amazing!'

Danny started to relax and enjoy the cool silky feel of the water. He stopped shuddering every time water weed stroked his skin. He noticed beautiful pale greeny-gold shafts of light filtering down from the dawn sun above and he swam up to break the skin of the water with his nose. His nostrils sprang open in the morning air and the scent of the pond rushed into them. It was rich and almost spicy, like earth and grass and mint. He bobbed back down under the water to find Josh drifting happily nearby. 'How come I don't have to go up more often to breathe, Josh?' he asked.

'Frogs are amazing,' said Josh. 'We can breathe through our nostrils like this . . . ' He kicked his powerful legs twice and his nose popped through the skin of the water and up into the morning air. Danny copied him, pulling in another fresh breath

through his small nostrils. Josh dropped down
again and he followed.

'Or . . .' went on Josh, ' . . . we can breathe
through our skin. That's what we're doing now,
while our nostrils are shut. Our skin absorbs
oxygen from the water. It's brilliant, isn't it?'

'Two ways to breathe!' said Danny.

'Three if you include the gills
at the tadpole stage,' said Josh.

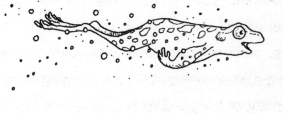

'Look at meeeeeeeeeeeeeee!' Charlie shot past
them again in a stream of bubbles and some small
whirling snails. 'This is better than Chessington
World of Adventure!!!'

'OK, OK! Slow down, Charlie!' Josh grabbed
one of her legs and she spun around in the water.

'What?' she demanded.

'Have you forgotten why we're down here?' said
Danny. 'We've got to get the key!'

'The key? Oh pooh!' grumbled Charlie. 'But this is so much FUN! Why don't we get Petty to spray us with loads more of that SWITCH stuff? We can just spend the rest of the camp time down here! Then we don't have to worry about Sergeant Major at all. This would be the BEST holiday!'

'No,' said Josh. 'We can't! For one thing everyone would go mad with worry. For another thing, sooner or later we'd have to get back on land and get some food. And then we might end up *being* food.'

'Come on,' said Danny. 'Start looking for the key! We've only got minutes left before Sergeant Major gets up and sees it's gone.'

'Look for the key fob,' said Josh. 'The bit hanging off the key. The red ink in it should be easy to see.'

'Shame we haven't got insect vision,' said Danny as they swam down to the murkier depths of the pond. 'When you're a bluebottle you can look all round at once. You can check out your proboscis and your bum at the same time.'

'Have you really been a fly?' marvelled Charlie.

'Yep. And done fly stuff,' said Danny. 'And trust

me—you don't want the details! You'd never eat a doughnut again.'

'No insects to worry about down here, though!' said Charlie, digging cheerfully through the silt, pondweed roots and clumps of algae. 'Eeeeeugh! Wrong . . .'

Several creatures shot out of the muck cloud she'd stirred up. Danny yelped. There were eight-legged, six-legged, even clawed things, rushing towards his face.

Josh chortled. 'They're just water mites and water fleas and freshwater shrimps. You can eat them if you like.'

It was a menu of horror for Danny. He shut his eyes (as far as he could—they didn't seem to have proper eyelids; just filmy things) until the minibeasts had swum past him.

'What's the time now, do you think?' Josh murmured. He was getting anxious. They'd spent far too much time having froggy fun. Danny checked his wrist automatically, before realizing his watch wasn't there—just a slender freckled greeny-brown hand.

'I've got it! I've got it!' cried Charlie. 'Woohoo!' She had scooped up the key and the fob and was wearing the ring that connected them on one arm, like a bangle. 'Let's hop up onto the bank then, so Petty can change us back.'

They swam for the surface but Charlie paused mid kick. 'Hang on though . . . ' she said, her froggy face creasing with concern. 'What happens when we switch back? Are we all going to be starkers? Because that is something I DON'T want to see before breakfast!'

'No, we'll be fine,' said Josh. 'All our clothes get SWITCHed too. Petty says the cellular hijack just takes them with us. We've never come back starkers yet, have we, Danny?'

'Nope,' said Danny. 'Squashed, upside down, burnt eyebrows . . . but not starkers.'

'Good-oh!' chirruped Charlie. 'Because I'm definitely SWITCHing again! It's the best fun EVER.'

'Look . . . it's not all fun,' warned Josh. 'Sometimes it can be really dangerous.'

'Oh, you're just SAYING that because you want to stop me because I'm a girl!' scoffed Charlie.

And that's when the sword shot down through the water.

Seeing Red

A second later there was proof that frogs can scream. Charlie made the most terrifying screech as she was snagged down through the water at lightning speed. Before Josh and Danny could do more than blink she was gone; plunged away into the dark depths. The shaft of the sword plummeted with her and then, to Josh and Danny's horror, a plume of red came bubbling up towards them.

Josh tried to shut his eyes. He realized, with a wave of sickness, what they were seeing. He had watched a heron hunting once before, on an early morning outing with his Wild Things club. The heron had stood motionless for nearly half an hour before it suddenly turned into a vicious killing machine, driving its skewer-like beak into the water in a blur of speed and pulling it out with

a writhing, bleeding fish speared on it. A living kebab.

Charlie, he realized, with a cold thud in his heart, had just become a heron's breakfast.

Even as these thoughts fled through his brain, the huge sword was moving fast back up through the water. Something was indeed skewered on its beak. Something bleeding red through the water. Something not moving. The beak and the bleeding body vanished, leaving only a few wisps of crimson, wafting and dissolving eerily through the water.

Josh felt Danny put his webbed hand on his shoulder. 'Tell me this isn't happening, Josh,' he whimpered. How would they ever explain how Charlie had died? Nobody would believe it. And Petty would never get involved at all. She would deny everything.

Josh and Danny were so shocked they forgot to move—even though they could very well be next on the menu. They stared vacantly ahead, desperately trying to make sense of what had just happened.

'Wha-what was that?' said Danny, at last.

'Heron,' croaked Josh. 'It would have been fast. She wouldn't have known much about it.'

'I really liked her,' said Danny, his head drooping in sorrow. 'She was brilliant fun. The most fun girl I've ever met.'

'Aaaah, that's really nice of you to say so,' said Charlie. 'I like you guys too.'

'BAAAAAA?!' shrieked Danny. And Josh agreed.

'WAAAAAA?!' Danny added. Josh went along with that.

Charlie grinned at them. 'That was scary!' she said. 'Blimey! You said nothing in the pond would try to eat us, Josh.'

'Bu—wha—cah . . . ?' Josh blinked several times and felt a huge surge of relief pump up through him. 'Well . . . there isn't anything in the pond . . . but there's always something above it. I should have remembered the heron!'

'You're ALIVE!' yelled Danny, full of joy. 'But what about all the blood? We saw blood going everywhere!'

'Nah,' laughed Charlie. 'That was the red ink from inside Sergeant Major's key fob. Gave me a bit of a fright too. That daggery beak missed me by a millimetre—it went for the fob instead.'

'Oh no—does that mean the key's gone?' Danny gulped and stared up through the water.

'Nope,' said Charlie, shaking her right arm. The key and the key ring were still on it. 'The plastic broke off the ring. That's all.'

'We've got to get out of here and get Petty to change us back,' said Josh. 'I can't see the heron out there but he could still be hunting. He wouldn't have liked the taste of that key fob.'

'But if we hop up to the surface, won't he eat us?' Danny gulped.

'We'll go up under
the lily pads,' said Josh,
pointing across to what looked
like a flotilla of rounded dark green rafts on part of
the surface of the pond. 'We can pop up through
them and then jump into the pond plants at the
edge. With any luck he won't see us. We can't
wait down here any longer.'

They swam in formation to the rafts, which
were held together by a snaky network of
underwater stems. Chinks of bright morning light
streamed down through the gaps between them.

The moment Josh pushed his eyes up through
the skin of water he saw Petty standing up, waving
her hands and going 'Raaah!'

The heron flapped away above them.

Plop! Plop! Plop! Three frogs arrived at Petty's feet, one of them slightly clumsily, with a heavy metal key on its shiny wet wrist.

'Well done!' hissed Petty, kneeling down, easing the key off Charlie's wrist and spraying them all with some more yellowy stuff. The antidote! They waited expectantly, moving away from the edge of the pond. After a few seconds, nothing had happened.

'Oh pee, porridge and poo!' muttered Petty, her gigantic face screwing up in annoyance. 'I've brought the wrong bottle out! That's another bottle of froggy AMPHISWITCH. Sorry! You'll just have to wait to SWITCH back when it wears off.'

The frogs started gesturing at Petty in annoyance. 'I know! I know!' she said, looking at her watch. It was just five minutes to six. 'Not to worry—*I'll* get the games in the cupboard and key back on the hook.' She shoved the key in her pocket, gathered up the games and was just about to dash off when Josh landed heavily on her foot and pointed up into the trees above them. The heron was there, perched elegantly on a branch, his blue-grey wings folded and gleaming softly in the morning sun . . . just waiting for the human to depart so he could resume his froggy feast.

'Aaah. Yes. Perhaps you'd better come with me,' said Petty. 'Come along—hop to it.'

Snacks and Snores

If anybody had been awake to see it they
would have been amazed at the sight of a stout
pensioner, clutching a stack of kids' gadgety
games, dashing across a field like a sprinter,
accompanied by three frogs, leaping ahead of her
in energetic bounds.

'Wheeeeeeee!' Charlie had quite got over her
near death experience and was hugely enjoying the
fun. So were Josh and Danny. Their back legs were
immensely powerful and catapulted them about
half a metre with each push off.

'Oooh—yum!' said Charlie, halfway through
a leap. Danny glanced across to see some long
spindly legs and a wing wriggling out of the side
of her mouth. 'What was that?' she asked. 'It
was like popcorn in the air! Who's throwing me
popcorn?!'

'That would be a mayfly,' said Josh, narrowly
avoiding Petty's wellington boot.

'Eeeeugh!' shuddered Danny. But a second later
his tongue shot out of his mouth at incredible
speed and collected another winged snack.
Crunch! Munch! It was gone before he realized
it. And it tasted good! Like a Wotsit. 'Aaaaargh! I
can't believe I just did that!' croaked Danny, while
Charlie whooped with delight.

'We're here!' said Petty and they all plopped onto the wooden deck of the office cabin. Petty crept into the office and took the games straight to the confiscation cupboard. Josh, Danny and Charlie landed with three small damp thuds on the desk and watched Petty carefully unlock the door and place the games inside. Up on the wall the clock showed it was three minutes to Sergeant Major's six o'clock alarm . . .

'Hurry UP, Petty,' whispered Josh.

Petty relocked the cupboard. Then she very carefully pushed open the door into the bunk room behind the office. At once a gale of snores could be heard. Petty crept in, a huge silhouette in the dim light, and the three frogs followed, trying hard not to plop too loudly on the wooden floor.

Sergeant Major lay on his side, snug in his pyjamas under a duvet, snoring loudly. His back was turned to them as Petty reached across to hang the key on the wall hook just above the head end of his bed. On the bedside table the digital clock read 5.58 a.m. As the amphibian crew stared at it, shivering with nerves, it flicked to 5.59 a.m.

'Hurry!' Charlie couldn't help whispering, jumping up in the air with anxiety. Unfortunately she landed with a loud slap exactly in the lull between snores. Sergeant Major snorted, snuffled, and energetically turned over. Petty Potts hit the deck like an athlete, dropping the key with a loud thud—just as Sergeant Major's eyes blearily opened. She crouched low down on his mat and scrunched up her face, waiting for the awful moment of discovery, while three frogs sat in a row behind her, their mouths hanging open in horror. For a few seconds there was silence.

Then, the alarm went off.

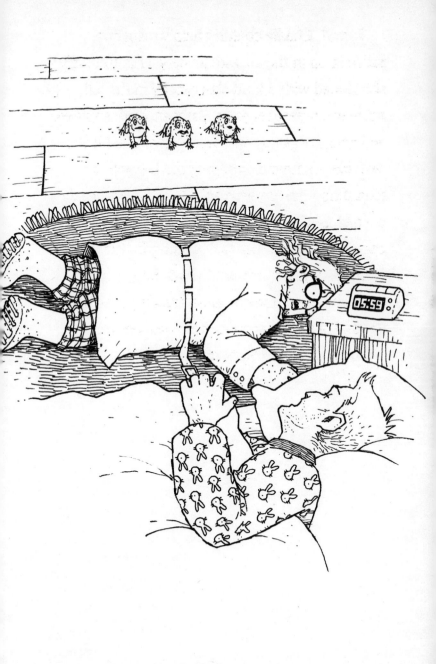

Snoozy, Oozy, Woozy

·

In the shadow of Petty's crouching backside Josh
and Danny slammed their hands across their
wide mouths to stop a scream of terror shooting
out. Charlie put hers over her big eyes . . . and
a high-pitched squeak did make it out of her
mouth—but fortunately the shrill beeping of the
alarm hid it. Sergeant Major grunted and began
slapping across to the bedside table to shut off the
noise. His slappy hand missed Petty's dismayed
face by a centimetre and eventually hit the clock.
It fell into silence again and Danny, peering past
Petty, noticed that a digital word had sprung up
above the numbers which now read 6.00 a.m.
It said 'SNOOZE'. Snooze? That meant another
five minutes, didn't it? Yes! Sergeant Major rolled
onto his back and made grunty, slurpy noises as

his tongue gradually unstuck from the roof of his mouth and his jaw fell open. His eyes were shut. He was going to have a snooze!

Danny could stand it no longer. He grabbed the key from the floor, jumped up onto Petty's shoulder and then leapt for the hook. Employing all his basketball skills, he stretched his arms out and threw the key at just the right angle so that the little metal ring would drop down over the hook. Half a second later there was a ringing metallic clink as he scored.

'Yeeeeessssssss!' Charlie and Josh couldn't help shouting. Then 'Noooooooo!' as Danny landed on Sergeant Major's face, one leg in his open mouth.

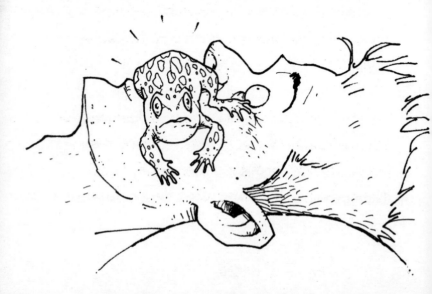

What followed was a bit mad. Sergeant Major bawled 'Plawaaa!' and shot up in bed, scrabbling at his face and thwacking Danny down onto the duvet. Danny screamed loudly, and then, realizing that he had to keep the man's attention while Petty crawled out of the room, he did a little dance. He did a hand jive and a shimmy across the duvet while Sergeant Major stared at him in astonishment, his mouth still wide open and his eyes bulging. He looked like a frog himself. He didn't see the old lady shuffling across his floor on her hands and knees with two leaping escorts. He was far too busy wondering how a frog had learned to disco dance.

Finally the alarm went off again, and in the second his audience glanced away, Danny hopped it.

'We DID it!' Charlie jumped up and down outside the girls' cabin. 'We got the games back in the cupboard! We got the key back on the hook! Nobody will ever know! I won't be sent home!'

'No,' said Josh. 'Nobody will notice anything strange at all, will they?'

'Aah,' said Charlie, noticing she was still a frog. 'But it will wear off soon, won't it?'

'I can't find my antidote,' Petty was whispering, hoarsely, bending down from above. 'You'll just have to get back into bed, all of you, and wait for it to wear off. It shouldn't be more than twenty minutes. I'll see you at breakfast!'

And she was gone.

'This has been the best adventure ever!' said Charlie. 'See ya!' She jumped into the cabin through an open window and as no girly screams followed, Josh and Danny guessed nobody had seen her get back into bed.

They got back into their own beds the same way and happily neither Callum nor Sayid noticed, being fast asleep.

It seemed like only minutes later that they were all getting up for breakfast, although it was 7.30 a.m. Josh and Danny got into their clothes and put wellington boots on very quickly while the others weren't looking. They hurried into breakfast and sat down at Charlie's table.

'Um . . . everything . . . OK?' hissed Josh as Charlie dolloped golden syrup on her porridge.

'Mostly OK,' said Charlie. They looked down and saw that she had wellingtons on too, even though it was a sunny day and everyone else was in sandals or trainers.

'You too?' said Danny, in a low voice.

'Yep . . . but it'll wear off soon . . . won't it?' Charlie eased her feet out of the wellies and the boys glanced down to see the truth beneath the table.

Charlie's feet were still frog coloured and frog shaped, complete with webbed toes—exactly like Danny's and Josh's.

'Yeah . . . ' said Danny, reaching for the toast. 'It'll wear off. The after-effects always do— although they've never been this obvious before.'

Josh grinned. 'Yeah . . . don't worry. It'll be fine. No need to get all jumpy.'

Newt Nemesis

CONTENTS

Toe Trouble

SOCKS. And not just any socks. LONG socks. THICK socks. HOT socks. Socks that had no business being dragged up the legs of any normal person on a day like this.

Camp counsellor Amy Jessup was a little worried.

The kids at Outdoor Action Camp were cool. Fashionable. They had the latest footwear and funky messy hair cuts. One of the girls even had a tattoo, it was rumoured (although others claimed it was just a lick and stick job out of a *Spiderman* magazine).

Looking at them, there was no doubt, thought Amy, that they were up-to-the-minute twenty-first century kids.

'So what's with the 1950s Boy Scout SOCKS?'

she murmured, aloud, staring at Josh and Danny and Charlie, the girl always getting up to mischief.

While all the other kids had got rid of their shoes and were wearing surfer style sandals or flip-flops—or going barefoot—these three were all wearing long grey socks, pulled up to their knees, and stout walking boots. And they weren't going anywhere near the lake or the shallow winding river where so much fun was being had in the hot sun with dinghies and rafts. Instead they were huddled under a large oak tree, whispering together.

'What are you three up to?' called out Amy as she strode towards them. 'Don't you want to play in the water? It's a perfect day for it . . . I'm surprised you're not mad keen to get your feet wet!'

'Ummm,' said Josh, while Danny and Charlie plastered wide grins across their faces so fast, Amy was even more suspicious.

'Yeah, well . . . actually,' said Josh, scratching his short tufty fair hair nervously. 'We were wondering about building a tree house—up there!' He pointed up into the impossibly high branches of the oak tree.

'Josh, you'd need mountaineering gear to get up this one.' Amy laughed. She was nice, sturdy and jolly with her wavy brown hair always in a pony tail, and everyone at Outdoor Action Camp liked her.

'OK—we'll go and find a better tree!' said Charlie with a bright smile and she grabbed Josh's and Danny's arms and tugged them away while Amy shook her head and shrugged. Kids. Weird. In so many ways.

And these three were weirder than most. As

soon as they got round the far side of a small clump of holly bushes, Josh, Danny and Charlie sat down and sighed. 'Let's look again,' said Charlie after a few seconds. 'It might have worn off a bit.'

They all rolled their long grey knee socks down to their boots. It looked as if they'd all recently smacked their ankles with cricket bats. The skin was greeny-brown, as if it was covered in a massive bruise. A bit weird.

Danny unlaced his boots first and pulled them off with a groan of relief. Then the rolled-down socks followed, allowing his poor cramped feet to spread out. Soon all three had their boots off and weird just went right off the superweirdofallweirdness scale.

All of them had perfectly formed frogs' feet.

Josh flexed his webbed toes. 'Aaaah, that's better.'

'How long is this going to go on?' asked Charlie, anxiously chewing on one of her many beaded dark plaits. 'We can't hide these for ever. These boots are killing me. Why can't I just wear my wellies? There's more room!'

'We're trying not to stand out, remember?'
Josh sighed. 'On a hot dry day we can just about
explain socks and ankle boots . . . but wellingtons?
I don't think so.'

'And I SOOOOO want to get them wet,'
moaned Charlie, her shiny green flippers waggling
up and down. 'They belong in water! Can't we just
creep into the river and have a little paddle? It'll be
lovely and cool and sloshy and slippy . . .'

' . . . and funny and strange and then shouty
and screamy,' pointed out Danny. 'And then
doctory and ambulancey and FREAK SHOWY!'

'Fair point,' admitted Charlie. 'But what if they
never change back? We'll get found out sooner or
later . . . and then what will we tell people?'

'Oh, I dunno,' said Danny, rubbing his green ankles vigorously. 'The truth?'

'What?' said Charlie. 'That your next door neighbour, who seems like a nice old lady, is actually a bonkers genius scientist with a SWITCH spray for turning humans into creatures . . . ? And that she turned us into frogs yesterday? And this is . . . just an after-effect? Oh. OK then. Nothing to worry about. Yeah—I'm sure they'll all believe THAT!'

'Well, trouble is . . . ' said Danny, picking a small black beetle out of his scruffy, spikey fair hair and absent-mindedly eating it, ' . . . there's nothing else that makes any better sense, is there?'

'Petty Potts MUST have the antidote spray!' said Charlie. 'I can't believe she just lost it! She has to find it and change us back properly. I want to go rafting and—'

'Well . . . actually . . . we did ask her to SWITCH us, didn't we? Begged her, in fact.' Josh could hardly believe these words were coming out of his mouth. Only a couple of weeks ago he and Danny had vowed solemnly that they would

NEVER let Petty Potts SWITCH them into anything ever again.

After a summer of being SWITCHed into spiders, insects and beetles, they'd really had enough of Petty's Serum Which Instigates Total Cellular Hijack. Their cells had been hijacked way too many times.

'I can't believe we really begged her to SWITCH us, this time,' muttered Danny. 'I want to swim! It's not fair! She SWITCHed us into frogs—she should SWITCH us back again—properly!'

'We must have been mad,' said Josh.

'It was my fault,' sighed Charlie. 'I had to go and "borrow" that key, didn't I? And then lose it in the pond . . . '

'Yeah, but it was our idea to get Petty to spray us with FrogSWITCH and go frog diving for it,' admitted Danny. 'We couldn't let you get sent home in disgrace . . . '

'It's never taken this long to wear off before,' Josh went on. 'I guess it's because we got a double dose when she sprayed us with antidote which turned out to be more FrogSWITCH. I think my ankles are a *bit* less froggy. Hopefully they'll be normal again tomorrow. And maybe Danny will stop eating bugs.'

'I'm NOT eating bugs!' Danny shuddered, a long brown feeler stuck to his lip . 'As IF!' Danny loathed creepy-crawlies of all kinds. Even though he'd been quite a few.

'What side-effects did you get from being creepy-crawlies?' asked Charlie.

Danny grimaced. 'After we were house flies I kept trying to lick the bin. And I spat goo on my doughnut before eating it. And Josh's.'

'On *my* doughnut?' squawked Josh. 'You never told me that!'

'Sorry,' Danny shrugged.

'And when we'd been daddy-long-legs,' said Josh, after a short, doughnut-related freeze, 'you know . . . crane flies . . . we kept staring at lights, and sometimes even running at them, for days afterwards.'

'But those were all, kind of, in our heads,' added Danny. 'Not physical stuff, like this. And they all wore off after a week.'

'A week?' Charlie stared at her green shiny feet, aghast. 'You mean this could last another five or six days?'

'Maybe,' said Josh. 'Unless Petty uses her antidote on us. The right one this time. We need to find her and get her on her own. I haven't seen her all day—but her car's still in the car park so she must be around somewhere. Let's go and find her.' He started to pull the socks back on again.

Danny and Charlie did the same, with much grumpy muttering. It was hot and uncomfortable. Their froggy feet were flat and splayed out and didn't fit properly inside socks and boots. They had to crumple them up.

'Oi! You lot!' bellowed a familiar voice. They all jumped. Rather high. And Danny definitely croaked, but luckily Sergeant Major was shouting so loudly at them he didn't hear.

'What are you doing hiding away out here?' he yelled. His real name was Steve but everyone called him Sergeant Major because of all the shouting. He didn't seem to be able to talk in a normal voice.

'Just . . . looking at wildlife,' mumbled Josh. It was partly true.

'Well, hoppit back to the tepee!' roared Sergeant Major. 'We're practising the show—remember your parents are all coming to see it at tea time!'

'Ooh yes,' Charlie grinned. 'The show! I'm going to star in it, I am!'

The show was to have a caveman theme. They were all dressing up in caveman outfits and putting on a caveman dance. They'd made outfits out of old sacks and bits of fake fur earlier that week. Charlie had found an old bone in the kitchen bin and was planning to shove it in her hair. Danny and Josh had both made axes out of bits of flint and sticks and sticky tape.

Charlie suddenly gulped and looked worried, as they hurried after Sergeant Major. 'Erm . . . Sergea—I mean, Steve—what are we wearing on our feet? In the show . . . ?'

'Your feet?' bawled Sergeant Major. 'Nothing! Barefoot, as nature intended! Go straight to the tepee now, though. No costumes until the proper show.' Sergeant Major marched them into the tepee and there they had to practise the caveman dance in their hot, hot socks and boots while everyone else stayed cool in sandals or bare feet.

'Why've you got them on?' queried Sayid, one of the boys in Josh and Danny's dormitory cabin, as he pointed at Josh's boots with his papier mâché club.

'Um . . . verrucas,' said Josh.

'And me,' said Danny. 'Caught 'em off Josh.'

'And me,' said Charlie. 'Caught one on each foot from both of them. It's a verucca plague.'

'You are nutjobs,' commented Sayid and ran away, viciously clubbing an imaginary dinosaur (he wouldn't believe Josh when he told him there were no dinosaurs in caveman times).

Half an hour later Josh, Danny and Charlie were allowed back outside. They ran into a bush and checked their ankles.

Still.

Very.

Green.

'Mum and Dad will be here in two hours!' moaned Josh, peering down inside his socks in horror. 'I don't think they'll be pleased to find we're semi-aquatic mutants. We have to find Petty NOW!'

Charlie and Danny and Josh gulped. Their eyes bulged a little. Small croaks of fear came from their throats. And Danny ate a fly.

Wrong Footed

'Aaaah,' said Petty, behind the canteen cabin an hour later. 'I see.'

Josh, Danny and Charlie were sockless and the shiny web-toed truth was hard to miss.

'You have frogs' legs,' said Petty, rather unnecessarily.

'Yesss! We have frogs' legs!' hissed Danny. 'What are you going to do about it?'

'Erm . . . strike a really good deal with a French restaurant?' smirked Petty, raising her shaggy grey eyebrows behind her slightly smeary round spectacles.

'This isn't flippin' FUNNY!' Josh stamped his froggy foot and Petty snorted with laughter.

'We've had to keep them hidden ever since we got up this morning!' said Charlie. 'In long socks and boots! We're roasting hot.' It was very warm where they were standing and the big wooden kitchen compost bin was sending out steam just behind them as the sun dried out yesterday's rain. 'But that's not the serious problem. The BIG problem is . . .'

'. . . Danny eating bugs?' queried Petty.

'I am NOT eating bugs!' squawked Danny. A wing and a green leg were stuck between his front teeth. 'Why does everyone keep saying that? I hate creepy-crawlies! If one even landed on me I'd rip it off me.'

'Sorry—was that rip it or ribbet?' Petty bit her lip.

'Yes—ribbet!' snapped Danny.

'You know, English frogs don't even say ribbet, really,' Josh reminded him.

'Oh will you shut up, you freaky little frog boffin!' snapped Danny.

'I can see we have a problem here,' said Petty.

'It's not just Danny,' said Charlie, glancing around to be sure nobody was within earshot. 'At tea time all our parents are coming to see us in the show and we're supposed to dance around like cavemen—with bare feet!'

'Aaaah,' said Petty, again.

'So you've GOT to get us the antidote!' said Josh. 'Or this could be really bad for all of us.'

Petty scratched her grey hair and frowned. 'It's normally worn off of its own accord by now,' she pondered.

'Yes—but you gave us a second FrogSWITCH dose, didn't you? While we were still froggy from the first dose,' said Danny. 'It did wear off after we hopped back into bed and went to sleep . . . but not properly. It must be the accidental double dose that did it.'

Petty opened her long red raincoat, which she had kept on all day despite the hot sun. In its lining were four bottles of AMPHISWITCH formula. One of them was meant to be antidote—but at least two of them had turned out to be FrogSWITCH. 'I wrote A for Antidote on one and A1, A2 and A3 for each of the different types of AMPHISWITCH sprays,' sighed Petty. 'A1 was frog and A2 was . . . oh, but look! The rain must have got into my coat and smeared them all about. I just don't know which one is AMPHISWITCH Antidote!'

'For a genius . . . ' said Danny, ' . . . you're quite dim. Exactly when did you think that identical bottles were a good idea?'

Petty glared at him. 'Look, when you have a brain as exceptional as mine, endlessly working on projects of astonishing brilliance, the small things sometimes have to make room for the big things.'

'Yes, well, this small thing has turned out to be pretty BIG for us, hasn't it?' said Josh. 'You've had another fun experiment—and we've all ended up with comedy legs! I don't know about Danny and Charlie but always coming first in long jump competitions isn't going to make up for the laughing and the pointing and the Channel 4 film crews!'

'The only thing to do,' murmured Petty, staring thoughtfully at the bottles, ' . . . is try them out.'

'Oh yeah! That'll help! Turn us into some other freaky amphibian!' Danny shook his head, shooting out his tongue as he did so and collecting an unwary moth from the side of the compost bin. He chewed sarcastically.

'Oh don't be such a fusspot,' said Petty, pulling

out the first bottle with a smeary A marked on it.
'If I get it wrong with this one . . .. and maybe even
the second and third one, as soon as I've found
the AMPHISWITCH antidote I can change you
back right away.'

'We've got no choice,' said Charlie. 'Our mums
and dads will be here in less than an hour!'

Petty nodded and sprayed Danny's froggy legs.
They all peered at the greeny-brown skin and
webbed toes and held their breath.

And then Danny was gone and a fat frog sat on
the ground in his place, giving Petty a cheesed off
glare from its pop-up eyes.

'Sooo,' said Petty. 'Not that one.' She pulled a
marker pen from another pocket and put a big F on
the bottle before setting it down next to Danny.
Then she got the next bottle out and sprayed it at
Charlie.

A few seconds later Charlie hopped over next to
Danny and giggled as she landed with a plop. She
was still rather excited about SWITCHing, even
though she'd nearly been eaten by a heron last
time.

'Aaah . . . ' said Petty. 'So two bottles are frog.' She marked the second bottle F2 and set it down next to Charlie. 'I didn't mean to bring two AMPHISWITCH Frog sprays . . . so this one . . . ' She held up another spray bottle. ' . . . is probably antidote.'

'Probably . . . ?' Josh didn't much like the sound of that probably. But before he could say anything else, Petty had sprayed him and in no time at all the world had gone HUGE again and he was down in the grass, tall green blades of it waving above him. He went to leap across to join Danny and Charlie but discovered that his back legs were rubbish. They didn't do anything! They only propelled him forward onto his nose. He stared at them in the reflection of a bit of broken glass beside the compost bin and noticed two things . . . one . . . his legs were black with white speckles and rather warty, not greeny-brown and smooth, and two, there was a neat row of stubby spines all down his back—ending in a long pointed tail.

'Whoa!' he called out. 'NOT a frog! I am NOT a frog.'

The grass waved violently and two large frogs suddenly landed in front of him.

'Oooh! Look at you!' marvelled Charlie. 'You're like a mini crocodile! Or a dragon!'

Josh was inspecting his belly now and grinned up at them. 'It's orange! How cool is that? I'm a Great Crested Newt!' He lifted up his four-fingered hand (or four-toed front foot; he wasn't sure) and marvelled at its black and bright orange stripes. 'Another kind of amphibian!'

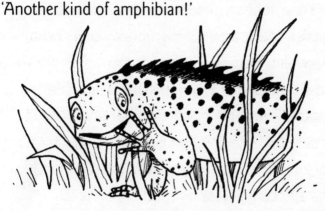

'You don't look all that crested to me,' observed Charlie. 'You've hardly got a crest at all. I certainly wouldn't call it great.'

'Nah—not much crestage this late in the year,' shrugged Josh. 'You should see a Great Crested in spring though—amazing! Like a mini stegosaurus!'

As they stared at Josh's not so great crest a waft of misty spray hit them and they all instinctively backed away from each other. If that was antidote they'd be springing back up to human size any second (and it could get a bit violent). They waited a while but nothing happened.

'Has she used them all?' wondered Charlie. 'That should have been antidote . . . shouldn't it?' Nearby, Petty's enormous hands were fumbling with the bottles (now looking the size of beer barrels) which were rolling around by her giant boots.

'She's probably just mixed them up again,' grunted Josh. 'She'll find it in a minute. I don't mind being a newt for a bit. Wish I could have longer like this. I'm special, you know! Guess what? I'm protected!'

'Protected? What, with, like, an invisible forcefield or something?' asked Danny, sucking on a sort of grey humbug with whirring legs which he'd failed to notice was a woodlouse.

'Invisible forcefield? I wish!' Josh grinned. 'No—I mean Great Crested Newts are a protected species. I'm rare, I am! Not allowed to be killed!'

'Eeeerm,' croaked Charlie. 'You might want to tell that to . . . him . . . ' Her pop-up froggy eyes had suddenly got so poppy-uppy they looked as if they might ping out of her head like marbles. She was keeping very still but the little patch of skin under her throat was quivering fast. Danny and Josh followed the direction of her glassy stare and tried not to scream.

Staring right at them from the foot of the compost bin, its long forked tongue quivering in the air, was a HUGE snake.

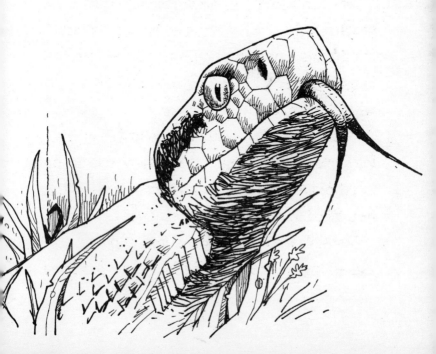

Wham, Bam, Fang You, Ma'am

'Oh pee, porridge and poo!' cursed Petty. The last spray had done nothing. It should have been either ToadSWITCH or the Antidote, but so far the two frogs and the great crested newt were still sitting there, having a little chat and most definitely not SWITCHing back to two boys and a girl.

She shook the bottle and peered at it in annoyance, squinting through the smears on her glasses. What was it? Then she unscrewed the top and peered inside. From the outside all the bottles looked the same—but inside she noticed it wasn't quite the same colour as usual . . . it looked a little . . . blue.

'Oh, Petty! You turbo-boosted, fuel-injected, twin-engined FOOL!' she snapped. 'This isn't SWITCH formula! It's your spectacles cleaning spray!'

Petty took off her spectacles and sprayed them, gave them a thorough wiping with her hanky and then put them back on. 'That's much better,' she remarked to the much more clearly viewed frogs and newt. 'Aaah. But now we have a problem . . . '

How was she going to get them SWITCHed back in time for the show? With NO antidote at all . . . ?

And then that little problem was upstaged by a much bigger one. A much longer one, too. Through her sparkly clean lenses, Petty suddenly noticed that Josh, Danny and Charlie were all sitting very very still and their little eyes were bulging and their little throats were quivering.

Then the long problem coiled its zigzag patterned body, raised its head and sent out a flickering forked tongue, tasting the air. Its scaly face drifted from side to side . . . once, twice, three times . . . and then its almond shaped eyes gleamed as it caught the unmistakable scent . . . of PREY. The head turned smoothly in the direction of Danny, Josh and Charlie and locked on to them. The tongue flickered once again.

And then it struck.

The movement was as fast as lightning and the frogs shot into the air at top speed. Charlie and Danny were gone in a heartbeat but Josh . . . Josh was a newt! Newts weren't exactly speedy even in water . . . much less on dry land! Josh was trying to struggle away across the mulchy stuff which had spilled from the compost bin, but the snake was rearing up its head, ready to strike again and Josh had NO CHANCE.

Petty flung herself towards the snake, meaning to grab it from behind and pin it down. For a broad-bottomed lady in her seventies she moved pretty fast—but not fast enough. In a flash the snake whipped its head round.

And drove its fangs right into her leg.

For a few seconds Josh just stood on a leaf,

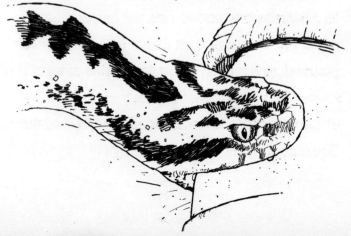

too shocked to move. As soon as the adder (he'd recognized its distinctive black zigzag patterned skin immediately) had reared up he'd known this was the end. Danny and Charlie had leapt away in half a second. They weren't abandoning him; they'd just done it out of pure instinct, forgetting that Josh was a newt—a slow, ungainly creature on land with no hope of escape.

Somewhere in the back of his mind he remembered that adders preferred mammals to amphibians . . . but by the way this one was looking at him, he was sure it was about to make an exception. The strike would come in a blur. The adder's fangs would inject venom in a second. It might try to swallow him there and then, but more likely it would just rest its cold brick-red eyes on him for a while as he tried to crawl away, waiting for his limbs to stop working as the paralysing agent in the venom took effect. Josh knew snakes preferred to digest their live prey when it wasn't kicking and screaming too much.

All this information occurred to Josh in about three seconds. Only yesterday Charlie had nearly

been eaten—and this summer he and Danny
had been on the menu for too many creatures to
mention—but now it really did look like the end.
A heron would have been better. Quicker.

And then there was a dark shadow and Petty's
walking boot crashed down a few inches away
from him. A moment later the adder struck; Josh
saw its jaws open wide and white fangs suddenly
emerge as if on springs. And it drove them right
into Petty's leg.

Petty gave a shriek and landed with an earth-
shuddering thud on her ample backside. The snake
fled back into the compost bin. As Josh stayed
frozen on his leaf, staring at the gigantic heap of
Petty Potts, two frogs leapt back in front of him.

'What happened?' gasped Charlie. 'We thought you were snake dinner!'

'No—it just had a munch of Petty instead,' said Josh, finally able to move again now that the terrifying predator had gone. At any other time he would have been thrilled to see an adder—but as a tiny newt, it had been utterly horrendous.

'She's been bitten?' gasped Danny. 'That's bad, isn't it?'

A very loud 'OW! OW! OW!' rang through the hot air above them. Petty was examining her calf. Two ruby red beads of blood were standing out on it through her thick beige tights.

'It's an adder,' said Josh. 'They are Britain's only venomous snake, but they can't kill you.' Another stream of ows erupted from Petty, whose face had gone rather red.

'Well,' went on Josh, 'not usually. I mean . . . death is very rare in humans.'

Petty suddenly rolled towards them and her big, big, BIG face loomed up close. 'Now listen!' she said, in a harsh whisper, the hairs in her foxhole sized nostrils trembling. 'I know you can't talk back

but wave your right . . .
er . . . hands . . .
if you can
understand me.'

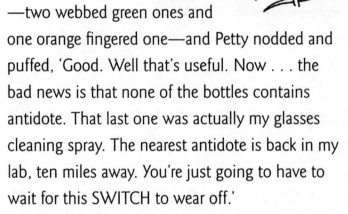

They all waved
their right hands
—two webbed green ones and
one orange fingered one—and Petty nodded and
puffed, 'Good. Well that's useful. Now . . . the
bad news is that none of the bottles contains
antidote. That last one was actually my glasses
cleaning spray. The nearest antidote is back in my
lab, ten miles away. You're just going to have to
wait for this SWITCH to wear off.'

'That was the BAD news,' said Danny. 'So
what's the good news? The good news?'

All of this came out as amphibious waving and
twitching to Petty, but she worked it out from the
frog's hopeful grin. Nodding and squinting down
at them through rather puffy eyes, she went on.
'The good news is . . . oh wait. There isn't any
good news. There's just badder news. I mean
worse news. I've been bitten by an adder.'

Josh sat back on his tail and pulled his speckly shoulders into an elaborate shrug. He wanted Petty to understand that though it might hurt, an adder bite wasn't any more dangerous than a bee sting.

Petty was breathing in a rather odd way. 'And what's badder than being bitten by an adder?' she went on, poetically. 'Well . . . having an adder venom allergy, probably. And . . . we tested lots of stuff on each other back in my old government scientist days and I learned two things. One, brazil nuts make me spew like a volcano . . . and two . . . I'm allergic to adder venom.'

Josh, Charlie and Danny stared at each other. 'What?' said Danny. 'So she's going to get a rash? Well, bad luck, Petty, but I think we've got a bit more to worry about than you!'

'No!' Charlie's froggy features crumpled with concern. 'You don't understand, Danny. She's— look at her—she's having a proper allergic reaction. My friend is allergic to bee stings. I was with her one day when she got stung and she got all puffed up and had to go to hospital. Look—Petty's going puffy!'

Petty was waving at them all now. 'Listen!' she rasped. 'Liiiiisten! I CAN'T MOVE! I can't get help because moving will pump the venom faster through my blood stream. You have to get my EPIPEN! My EPIPEN! It's in my cabin. On the chest of drawers beside my be-e-ed.'

Charlie nodded vigorously to show she understood. 'Danny—you come with me!' she said, suddenly taking charge. 'Josh, you're too slow. You stay here with Petty. We'll be back with the EpiPen as soon as we've found it. I know what they look like. My friend carries one all the time now.'

123

She and Danny leapt away towards the staff cabins, flinging themselves through the long grass until Josh couldn't see them. He stood looking at Petty, who had put one thumb up and was now peering at him through narrow slits in her puffed-up eyes.

'Well . . . done!' she gasped. 'Now . . . make sure . . . that brother of yours . . . saves my life, Josh. Don't forget . . . I'm a genius . . . the world . . . needs . . . geniuses . . . Or is that . . . geni-ii?'

'SHUT UP AND CONCENTRATE ON BREATHING!' yelled Josh but he knew Petty couldn't hear him at all.

He climbed up on Petty's arm, wondering if it was in any way possible for a dangerously ill human to be comforted by one slightly damp newt. Petty's puffed-up eyes were shut now and her face was looking swollen too.

'Huuurrry up, Danny and Charlie!' wailed Josh. 'Before it's too late!'

FETCH!

'We'll get there in no time,' called out Charlie as she and Danny leapt along in rainbow arcs amid the cool, damp, long grass at the back of the cabins. 'This is BRILLIANT! It's as good as swimming under water.'

'You should try GrasshopperSWITCH then,' called back Danny. 'A grasshopper can hop and sort of glide with little wings, about twenty times the length of its own body. Way more than a frog. Ooooh no. I just started to talk like a freaky little bug boffin!'

'No—it's cool! I love all this stuff,' shouted back Charlie as she leapt ahead of him.

'It was fantastic when me and Josh were grasshoppers,' went on Danny. 'Apart from him nearly getting eaten by a cat . . . and me nearly getting flattened with a maths book . . . Ah! Is this the staff bedrooms cabin?'

Charlie landed on a low wooden windowsill. Danny arrived next to her a second later and they both peered in through the glass, their hands sticking to it with a slight squelch.

'Is this the right room?' whispered Danny. He had no idea why he was whispering. Even if he talked normally no human would hear him.

Charlie stuck her buggy eyes up close to the glass. 'Naah. It's Amy's room,' she said. 'And that means . . . Petty's room must be round the front.'

'How do you know?' asked Danny.

'Oh, I've had a look in all their rooms.' Charlie grinned.

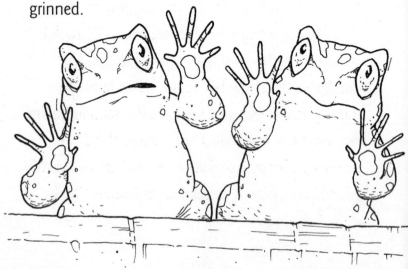

'But—you're not allowed in their rooms!' Danny was shocked. *He* was usually the one being told to behave.

'Oh, I don't touch anything!' said Charlie. 'I'm just curious! And you have to feed your curiosity, that's what my dad says . . .'

She hurled herself merrily off the windowsill. 'Come on!' she yelled back to Danny. 'Remember it's a matter of life and death!'

They sprang energetically round to the front of the building. Too energetically. As they jumped out from the narrow alleyway that ran between this and the neighbouring cabin, Charlie hit the gravelly ground with a splat and then screamed. Really screamed! Loud enough for anyone to hear. Rolling straight for her was an ENORMOUS mud-spattered tyre. Danny lurched across to Charlie, grabbed her left leg in his wide mouth and pulled her out of the way half a second before the enormous tyre rolled over where she'd been, sending up a spray of dust and small bits of gravel. It could so easily have been small bits of Charlie.

'It's OK! You're safe!' said Danny as Charlie stared up, her froggy mouth gaping open with horror and her eyes ready to pop out of their bulgy sockets. 'It's OK!' repeated Danny. He'd tugged her into a clump of long grass so whatever it was that had gone past, they were safe for the moment. But Charlie didn't look as if she felt safe. She was still gaping and staring and her throat was quivering at top speed.

Danny glanced sideways and saw that the tyre had rolled past now and come to a stop. It belonged to a car—a Beetle. A shiny black one. It seemed familiar. Its passenger door opened and there was a flurry of movement. Of course— parents must be arriving for the show! It was Mum's car!

Charlie suddenly started screaming again.

'What is it?' said Danny, thinking he might have to slap her cheek.

'It's—THAAAAAAT!' screamed Charlie and now Danny felt a blast of warm, meat-scented air just behind him. He looked round and saw something truly horrific.

It was a HUGE MOUTH. And that was familiar too. It belonged to his dog—Piddle. A small, scruffy black and white terrier who LOVED chasing things. And catching things. And Piddle was LOVING a new game he'd just thought up—called CATCH THE JUMPY THINGS.

'Piddle! PIDDLE! STAY!' bellowed Danny as a wobbly pink tongue and yellowy white fangs in black gums suddenly plunged towards them.

One second later Charlie and Danny sprang high into the air. Two seconds later, Danny found himself in Piddle's mouth.

Canine Catastrophe

It was warm and soggy and bouncy inside Piddle's mouth—and very smelly.

'Bleeuch! Dog breath!' gurgled Danny as he was jogged up and down on his pet's tongue. He wrapped his froggy fingers tightly around the two yellowy white lower canine teeth which rose up from the front corners of Piddle's mouth like ivory posts. Luckily they weren't too clean and the sticky pads on his fingers were able to grip on to the gunge. If he held on tightly enough he might not get swallowed.

'PIDDLE! SPIT ME OUT!' bawled Danny.

Piddle felt some tickly vibrations through the top of his mouth. He coughed and Danny was jerked forwards and then backwards towards the dark red cavern at the back of Piddle's mouth.

'NOOOOOOO!' shrieked Danny as his hands lost their grip on Piddle's teeth. He pushed hard against Piddle's blunt back molars with his powerful feet and legs and managed to shoot forward again until his head was poking out between Piddle's fangy front canines, the small sharp incisors in between digging into his soft belly.

The outside air rushed against his face and Danny realized that Piddle was galloping about excitedly, the way he always did when he'd caught something. The ground and the sky and the cabins and the car were all blurring into each other as Danny was swung up and down violently. His legs and feet were still held tight between the slurpy tongue and the hard ridges of skin on the roof of Piddle's mouth. Piddle was sucking a frog!

'PIDDLE!' Danny yelled again. 'That is DISGUSTING!'

Mind you, chewing a frog would be even more disgusting. And Piddle did LOVE *chewing* stuff. Danny realized it was quite likely that his eight years on the earth might end in being munched to death by his own lovable pet terrier.

He dragged in a HUGE breath of air and bellowed, 'PIDDLE! PIDDLE! DROP! DROP IT! DROP IT!'

Piddle suddenly stopped leaping about and came to a surprised halt. He wasn't the most obedient dog but he usually did as he was told by his family . . . eventually. And it really DID sound as if one of them had just told him to DROP IT.

Piddle put his innocent face on and tilted his head in a winning way. Sometimes this won him a few extra seconds of playtime with whatever it was he had got.

'Piiiiiddle!' came the voice again. Confusingly, from INSIDE his head.

Well . . . he *would* put the jumpy green thing down. Like a good dog. Very soon. But first . . . he wanted just a *little* chew.

Danny let out a froggy scream as Piddle sat back on his haunches and released the sucky grip on his back legs, only to flip his tongue sideways and swiftly shove them between a set of powerful top and bottom grinding teeth.

At this point another jumpy thing suddenly landed with a splat on Piddle's nose and punched him in the eye. He let out an affronted bark and the two jumpy things spun out from his shaking snout and landed in the grass. Piddle sneezed twice and when he next looked, to his great disappointment, his funny jumpy chew toys had vanished.

'Thank you! Thank you SO much!' spluttered Danny. He and Charlie were crouching in the gap under the cabin, out of sight of Piddle. He felt his legs, gingerly, and was relieved to find he still had both—although there was a line of dents across his soft green belly, left by Piddle's incisors. 'I was just about to be frog crunch!' he whimpered.

'I know! It would have been soooo icky!' said Charlie.

'Icky? Icky?' squawked Danny.

'We haven't got time to wait here much longer!' hissed Charlie. 'Petty's puffing up by the second, remember! We HAVE to get into the cabin and get her EpiPen.'

Danny peered out nervously between the tufts of weed that screened them from the outside world. Piddle was now running away towards the tepee where the show was on. He could make out his mum and dad now, too. Dad had called Piddle away and was putting him on the lead.

'OK—it's now or never!' he gulped and they sprang back out into the hot sun and turned to look up at the window.

'Top window's open,' said Charlie and leapt up to the sill. 'I think I can make it. Can you?'

'Yes, of course!' said Danny. He wasn't having a girl showing him up—even if she *had* just rescued him from the jaws of death.

They both leapt again up to the open top window.

'I can see the EpiPen! I can see it!' said Charlie and hopped straight onto Petty's bedside table.

The pen, containing Petty's medicine in a syringe, was big. It lay next to the lens wipe cloth for her spectacles. Although not very heavy, it was awkward. 'How are we going to get it back?' wondered Danny. 'It's too long to hold in our mouths. And how are we ever going to inject her?'

Charlie gazed around and then her eyes fell on something interesting next to the lens wipe. 'I think I have an idea,' she said.

Fun With Prickles

Rustle. Rustle-rustle. Click. Rustle . . .

It wasn't the scariest of noises really. And above Petty's whistly breathing he could hardly hear it. But Josh *was* scared as he perched on Petty's arm. Very scared. Something was coming out of the compost bin . . .

'Ooooh! Hurry up, Danny! Get a move on, Charlie!' wailed Josh. How he wished he'd been SWITCHed into a frog. At least he would have had a fighting chance then. A frog could leap away from danger in a heartbeat, but not a slow, lumbering newt.

Newts, he realized glumly, were a bit pants.

Rustle. Rustle-rustle. Click . . . click . . .

'Oh, PETTY! Wake UP!' he yelled, but Petty, who was now inflated like a rather unattractive bouncy castle, wasn't going anywhere. What was even more scary was the thought that, at any time, the whistly breathing could just stop altogether. He and Danny had never been that fond of Petty—and often quite cross with her. She had played with their health and safety far too often!

But he realized he would truly miss her if she was no longer footling about in her under-garden lab next door. She was amazing, really. Whacky. Eccentric. Brilliant. Very possibly insane. There would never be another next-door neighbour like her.

Rustle. Scrape. Suddenly the thing came out of the compost bin at a run. It was brown, spiky, with shoe-button eyes, a twitching sharp snout and a hungry expression. And it was running straight for him.

Josh tried to scuttle round into Petty's armpit but all he did was fall over, with a damp plop, right in the path of the oncoming beast. Two seconds later he was in its jaws.

Hedgehogs. Such cute things. He'd always found them SO endearing. This one wasn't endearing at all. Its teeth were stabbing into his orange belly as his little arms and legs and tail waved frantically in the air. Once again Josh prepared to exit from the world as a crunchy snack.

But then he felt an odd coolness pass across his back and a chemical smell wafted around him.

A second later the hedgehog gave an explosive shudder and spat him out in a spray of foam. It gasped and sneezed and snapped, 'Newts! Why DO I bother? Yeeeuch!'

Josh rolled over in the grass and gaped up at the predator which was now wiping furiously at its snout. Foamy dribbly snot stuff was flying in all directions. Then Josh remembered. 'HA! HA!' he chortled. 'I squeezed out toxin through my skin! You got a mouthful of yuck! YAY! Newts ROCK!'

'Don't push your luck, ugly,' muttered the hedgehog, spitting out frothy blobs.

Josh didn't. He staggered back underneath Petty's arm.

'Eeeeurgh! Human!' shrieked the hedgehog, noticing Petty for the first time. It ran away at speed. Josh looked at his bleeding belly and checked for entrails. No. It was just a light skin wound this time. But the next thing that came along might not be so picky . . .

Spray You, Spray Me

'It IS! I bet you it IS!' said Charlie, jumping up and down next to the familiar white spray bottle.

'It could be anything,' said Danny, eyeing the bottle with mistrust. 'It could be SpiderSWITCH . . . ' he shuddered. 'And then we'd be even worse off than now!'

'But look—remember—when Petty SWITCHed us all she said she'd mixed up one of the bottles with her lens cleaning spray for her glasses!' explained Charlie. 'So if she had the wrong bottle in her coat, she must have mixed it up with the right bottle. The antidote bottle. And this one is right here next to her lens wipe cloth! It's ANTIDOTE! I know it is!'

Danny gulped. 'Or it could be ToadSWITCH. She lost that one too.'

'Only one way to find out,' said Charlie.

'OK,' sighed Danny. 'I'll hold it in front of my face and you—jump on the spray button!'

He grabbed the bottle and positioned the nozzle side in front of his face. He shut his eyes. 'GO!'

Charlie jumped up and landed both her arms with force on the spray button. Danny closed his mouth and nostrils too and felt the cool spray land on him.

He felt a familiar tingle. 'Better move out of the—'

'—WAY!' Danny shot up the walls and nearly hit his head on the ceiling. Well—it felt that way. In fact he was just his usual boy size, sprawling across the wooden floor. As he lay there, dazed, a frog hopped up on his chest—and went on hopping.

He didn't need a translator to know that Charlie was shouting, 'SWITCH ME now! SWITCH ME!'

'Oh look! It's Danny! Danny—over here!' called Mum as her son hurtled past with a girl she hadn't met before.

'Can't stop!' yelled Danny. 'Saving a life!'

'OK, dear!' laughed Mum. 'Where's Josh?'

'Josh is a newt!' yelled back their son.

Mum smiled at Dad. 'Those boys! Always living in a fantasy world!'

Petty didn't look good when they got to her. Her face and neck and legs and arms were all swollen and her skin looked mottled and purple.

Charlie lost no time. She pulled the cap off the EpiPen and, like her friend had shown her, drove the spiky bit hard into Petty's leg, just above the snake bite.

'Is that it? Is she going to get better?' asked Danny, peering down at Petty in alarm.

He got his answer four tense minutes later. Petty's puffiness began to subside very quickly and then her eyes opened and then the whistly noise went out of her breathing. After ten minutes she was sitting up.

'You took your time!' she said. 'I was nearly DEAD!'

'Yeah, well—so were we!' said Danny. He glanced back at Charlie and then noticed that Josh wasn't there. 'Hang on! Where's Josh? Where is he?'

'Um . . . I'm not sure . . . ' said Petty, looking a little awkward. 'But I think he may have been eaten by a hedgehog.'

'WHAT?!' yelled Danny. He sank to his knees, horror struck.

'He might not have been,' said Petty. 'I couldn't really see much. He was just behind me. I was NEARLY DEAD myself, you know.'

'This isn't a HOW NEARLY DEAD I'VE BEEN TODAY competition!' screeched Danny, swiping through the long grass desperately. 'JOSH! JOSH! Where are you?!'

'Stand back,' said Charlie. 'And stand still! You might have just stamped on him!'

Danny peered at the soles of his feet in horror, but found no sign of newt squish on them. His heart thundered in his chest as he looked desperately around. Had he lost his twin? How would he ever explain this to Mum and Dad? How would he ever cope with spiders under his bed without Josh? He gulped.

Then Charlie stepped carefully forward and sent a long spray of SWITCH Antidote into the grass. Then another long spray. Then another.

FWUMP! Josh suddenly elbowed Petty hard in the ear.

'Aaargh!' she yelled. 'MIND OUT! Don't you know I was NEARLY DEAD?!'

'Well I got chewed by a hedgehog!' announced Josh. But he jumped to his feet and gave Charlie and Danny a joint hug. 'We're all ALIVE!' he grinned.

'Yes!' beamed Charlie. She looked at her watch. 'And we've got just under a minute to get to the tepee and do the show!'

Prehistoric Pogo

'Hurry up! Hurry up!' hissed Amy as soon as she saw Charlie, Danny and Josh running towards the tepee. 'Everyone's here and Sergeant Ma—I mean, Steve, is furious you're holding everything up!'

They flung themselves into their costumes, with great relief that their legs and feet were normal again. One minute later they rushed to the end of the line-up of caveman dancers. Nobody would have noticed they were late, thought Danny. Nobody would notice anything unusual at all.

Even Petty, looking perfectly normal again and not remotely puffy or nearly dead, had taken a seat among the parents. Mum and Dad waved. Piddle, carefully leashed and sitting nicely between Dad's knees, grinned and lolled his tongue about. Mum got out her camcorder.

Josh allowed himself to sigh with relief. It was all over. Then they began their dance.

After a few moments everyone started gasping and staring. Mouths fell open and camcorders and cameras dropped unheeded into laps.

Josh had fallen over and was sluggishly crawling across the tepee floor, waving his hands about in front of him in a wobbly way. He had no co-ordination at all. He guessed it was a SWITCH after-effect.

But that wasn't what the audience—and now most of the caveman dancers—were gasping and staring at. No. That would be Danny and Charlie, merrily leaping up and down and hitting their heads against the top of the tent pole every time . . .

'How can you do that?' yelled Sergeant Major. 'It's got to be four metres high!'

'Erm . . . ' said Petty. 'It's just the country air. It puts a spring in their step . . . '

DIARY ENTRY 635.2

SUBJECT: WORLD'S GREATEST GENIUS NEARLY LOST TO SCIENCE!

Back home now—and last week was a VERY close call! While working on my SWITCH experiment at the camp I got bitten by an adder and VERY NEARLY DIED thanks to my allergy. Imagine the loss to the world of science!!!

It was a good thing that Danny and Josh had made friends with that Charlie Wexford girl because she knew about EpiPens and how to use them or else I'd be a goner, for sure.

But aside from the happy situation of still being ALIVE, something else extraordinary happened. On the last day of camp Josh and Danny gave me the MISSING REPTOSWITCH CUBE! YES! They'd had it all along! It turns out they'd been upset about that 'stamping on a cockroach' incident and had decided I was too dangerous to possess the complete REPTOSWITCH code.

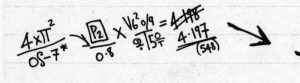

It's quite ridiculous, of course—being kept from my earth-shattering scientific destiny by two self-appointed eight-year-old Health & Safety executives!

But since we've all now saved each other's lives they changed their minds and decided I could have the last REPTOSWITCH cube after all.

HUZZAH! Now I have all SIX I can finally PERFECT the REPTOSWITCH spray and turn Josh and Danny into all kinds of reptiles! And this time I know they won't be able to resist helping . . . after all, what boy doesn't want to be an ALLIGATOR?!!!

HAHA! HAHAHAHA! BWAH-HA-HA-HAAAAA. (Note to self: Sinister cackling still not working on paper. Get audio recorder with echo effect?)

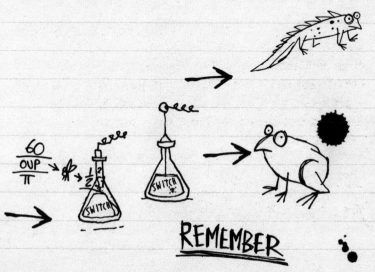

REMEMBER

GLOSSARY

Abdomen—The main part of an animal's body.

Allergy—A condition that some people have that makes their bodies react badly to things they eat or drink or touch or breathe in.

Amphibian—An animal that can live on land and in water.

Antidote—A medicine that can reverse the effects of a poison.

Bulbous—Fat, round or bulging.

Cellular—Something made from a group of living cells.

EpiPen—A medical device used to treat allergic reactions.

Hijack—To take control of something by force.

Incisors—Sharp-edged front teeth.

Mammals—Animals that give birth to live young and feed them with their own milk.

Molars—The wide teeth at the back of the jaw – used for chewing.

Predator—An animal that hunts other animals.

GLOSSARY

Prey—An animal that is hunted by another animal.

Proboscis—The long, sucking nose of an insect.

Reptiles—Cold-blooded animals. Lizards and snakes are reptiles.

Serum—Fluid used in science and for medical purposes.

Tepee—A cone-shaped tent, often made of canvas or animal skin.

Toxin—A poisonous substance.

Venom—Poison that can be squirted from the fangs of an animal to kill or stun its prey. Some snakes are venomous.

PLACES TO VISIT

Want to brush up on your bug knowledge?
Here's a list of places with special areas
dedicated to frogs and newts.

Slimbridge Wetland Centre

http://www.wwt.org.uk/visit-us/slimbridge/

Marwell Wildlife Park

http://www.marwell.org.uk/

Natural History Museum

http://www.nhm.ac.uk/

Remember, you don't need
to go far to find your favourite
creatures. Why not venture out
into your garden or the
park and see how many
different creatures
you can spot?

WEBSITES

Find out more about nature and wildlife
using the websites below.

http://www.bbc.co.uk/cbbc/wild/

http://www.nhm.ac.uk/kids-only/

http://kids.nationalgeographic.com/

http://www.switch-books.co.uk/

FUN AND GAMES

There are more games for you to play and
download free on the SWITCH website.
www.switch-books.co.uk

Word search

Search for the hidden words listed below:

DANNY   NEWT
JOSH   FROG
PIDDLE   ADDER
SPRAY   HERON
AMPHIBIAN   CHARLIE

D	A	N	N	Y	K	L	O	F	E
A	H	M	Z	C	F	J	R	B	L
N	D	I	P	R	O	Q	E	T	D
E	E	S	O	H	S	U	D	H	D
W	U	G	S	M	I	V	D	E	I
T	A	O	Y	T	H	B	A	L	P
K	J	C	H	A	R	L	I	E	X
S	B	N	I	O	D	T	G	A	N
H	E	R	O	N	M	F	J	V	N
G	A	D	A	K	S	P	R	A	Y

Answers on page 183

Spot the difference

These pictures *look* the same, but can you spot ten differences?

Answers on page 183

Memory test

Look at the 10 pictures for 15 seconds, then cover the page with your hand. With a pencil write down on a piece of paper as many pictures as you can remember – no peeking.

Give yourself 1 point for each picture you remember correctly.

Key

Newt

Petty Potts

Heron

Fish

Frog

Snake

Hedgehog

EpiPen

Piddle

Score:

0–3 points – Have another try

4–7 points – Good work!

8–10 points – You've got a brilliant memory!

Missing piece

Can you work out which piece of the puzzle is missing?

Answer on page 183

Which SWITCH character are you?

You prefer reading to listening to music

no .... yes

You'd rather find a football in the hedge than a hedgehog

You like entertaining your friends

no .... no

You love being outdoors

yes .... no

You are sporty

yes

You are very cheeky

no .... no

You like using a magnifying glass

yes .... yes

yes

DANNY
You are fun and fearless – except when it comes to creepy crawlies!

JOSH
You are a great explorer and like learning new things.

CHARLIE
Your friends love having you around because you are always full of energy.

Maze

Can you help Josh, Danny and Charlie to get through the maze to find the key?

Answer on page 184

Board game

You have been turned into a frog and have to get across the camp to Petty Potts's cabin to find the antidote. The player who gets there first is the winner.

For this game you will need one die, a tiddlywink (or something of a similar size) for each player and two or more players.

START 1	2	Uh-oh! Piddle wants to play! Hop back 1 square to get away. 3
6	You take a shortcut across the pond. Swim forward 2 squares. 5	4
7	You've been spotted by a heron! Hop back 2 squares to hide. 8	Wow! You do a really big jump. Move forward 2 squares. 9
12	11	10
Yum! You are distracted by a tasty mayfly snack. Miss a go. 13	14	FINISH Congratulations! You have made it to Petty Potts's cabin. 15

172

Who's who?

Can you find which frog is really Josh, Danny and Charlie?
Follow each path to find out.

Answer on page 185

Laugh-out-loud jokes!

Q) What happens when a frog's car
breaks down?
A) He gets toad away

Q) What kind of snake is good at Maths?
A) An Adder

Q) How does a frog feel when he has a
broken leg?
A) Unhoppy

Q) How do hedgehogs play leap-frog?
A) Very Carefully!

Q) Why did the frog make so
many mistakes?
A) It jumped to the wrong conclusions

Q) What do frogs say after
telling a joke?
A) Git-it? Git-it?

Q) Why did the frog go to the hospital?
A) He needed a 'hopperation'!

Q) Why wouldn't the snake go on the weighing machine?
A) Because he had his own scales

Q) What do snakes write at the bottom of their letters?
A) With love and hisses

Q) What's a snake's favourite dance?
A) Snake, rattle and roll

Q) What do toads drink?
A) Croaka-cola

Q) What kind of frog lives in a tree house?
A) A tree frog

Q) What do you get if you cross two snakes with a magic spell?
A) Addercadabra and abradacobra!

Quiz

1. What is Charlie's favourite thing?
a) Sitting still
b) Skateboarding
c) Bungee jumping

2. What is the name of the summer camp Danny, Josh and Charlie are at?
a) Outdoor Action Camp
b) Outdoor Adventure Camp
c) Action and Adventure Camp

3. In Frog Freak Out! Why do Josh, Danny and Charlie jump in the pond?
a) They fancy a swim
b) To get the key which Charlie dropped
c) To hide from Sergeant Major

4. In Frog Freak Out! what time does Sergeant Major's alarm go off?
a) 7:00
b) 5:30
c) 6:00

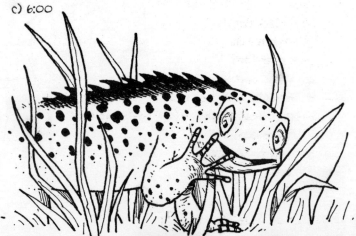

5. In chapter 1 of *Newt Nemesis*, why didn't Josh,
Danny and Charlie want to take their boots off?
a) They've got really smelly feet
b) It's a really cold day
c) They all have webbed feet

6. Who gets SWITCHed into a newt in *Newt Nemesis*?
a) Charlie
b) Josh
c) Piddle

7. What kind of car do Danny and Josh's parents
drive?
a) A black Beetle
b) A green Mini
c) A silver Ford

8. What do Josh, Danny and Charlie dress up as
for the show at the end of *Newt Nemesis*?
a) Amphibians
b) Mad scientists
c) Cavemen

Answer on page 184

Amazing Amphibians!

• Each species of frog has a different croak. Some species are named after the sound of their croaks — like bull frogs, sheep frogs, barking frogs and banjo frogs!

• A single toad can eat 10,000 insects in one summer.

• Newts can shed, or drop, their tails and legs if something grabs them. This helps them to escape.

• Frogs do not need to drink — they can take in water through their skin.

• The cane toad is the world's largest toad, and can grow to be as big as a dinner plate!

• Flying frogs actually glide. They spread their webbed toes really wide and the skin traps the air, like a parachute. Some tree frogs can glide for up to 15 metres.

• Some frogs can turn their stomachs inside out through their mouths and wipe it clean — handy if you've eaten something that tastes bad or is poisonous!

• Glass frogs have see-through skin, which means you can see the organs inside their bodies.

• The croak of a male natterjack toad can be heard several kilometres away.

How to Pond Dip

Equipment:
Large container — like a bucket or washing-up bowl
Small container — like a jam jar
Net
Spoon or tea-strainer

1. Half fill your large and small containers with pond water, and set away from the pond.

2. Using the net, slowly sweep a figure of 8 pattern in the water for about 10 seconds. Avoid the mud at the bottom and pond weed at the top as too much of either of these will make it difficult to see what you have caught.

3. Bring the net smoothly out of the water and empty the contents into the large container.

4. Put the net to one side, and use the spoon or strainer to move interesting minibeasts to the smaller container for closer examination.

Use a pen and paper to record what you have found.

Remember to return any creatures to the pond once you have finished looking at them.

DON'T FALL IN!
HEALTH AND SAFETY

• Always ask an adult to help
• Kneel rather than stand at the edge to keep your balance when dipping, and move away from the edge to look at what you have found.

True or false?

1. Dogs will foam at the mouth if they pick up a toad and try to eat it.

2. Frogs use their noses to smell.

3. Frogs do not have tails.

4. An adder is the only venomous snake in Britain.

5. Frogs lived on the earth way back when dinosaurs were alive.

6. Frogs can breathe through their skin.

7. An adder bite is more dangerous than a bee sting.

8. Frogs can eat their own skin.

9. Frog eggs are called frogsplat.

10. Some frogs swallow their eggs and keep them in their stomachs until the young frogs are ready to hop out.

Answers on page 185

Answers

Word search (page 166)

D	A	N	N	Y	K	L	O	F	E
A	H	M	Z	C	F	J	R	B	L
N	D	I	P	R	O	Q	E	T	D
E	E	S	O	H	S	U	D	H	D
W	U	G	S	M	I	V	D	E	I
T	A	O	Y	T	H	B	A	L	P
K	J	C	H	A	R	L	I	E	X
S	B	N	I	O	D	T	G	A	N
H	E	R	O	N	M	F	J	V	N
G	A	D	A	K	S	P	R	A	Y

Spot the difference (page 167)

Missing piece (page 169)

Answers

Maze (page 171)

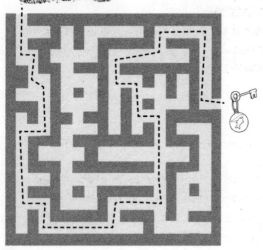

Frog Freak Out! Quiz (page 176)

1. C
2. A
3. B
4. C

5. C
6. B
7. A
8. C

Give yourself a point for every question you got right.

6-8 points — Excellent work! High-five for you!

3-5 points — Well done! You're as sharp as a snake's forked tongue!

0-2 points — Oh dear, looks like you got your frogs and toads all mixed up!
Read the story again before you give the quiz another go.

Answers

True or False (page 182)

1. T — because of the poison that comes from the glands on toads' skin.
2. F — they have a sense organ in the roof of their mouths instead.
3. T — only tadpoles do.
4. T
5. T
6. T
7. F — unless you're allergic to adder venom like Petty Potts!
8. T— Frogs shed their skin regularly. The frog wriggles out of it and then eats it. It contains nutrients which are good for the frog.
9. F — frog eggs are called frogspawn.
10. T — the male Darwin's frog in South America does this.

Who's Who?
(page 173)

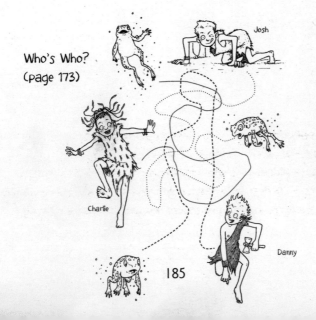

Josh

Charlie

Danny

185

About the author

Ali Sparkes grew up in the woods of Hampshire. Well –
not in the sense that she was raised by foxes after being
abandoned as a baby – she had parents, OK? Human
parents. But they used to let her run wild in the woods.
But not wild as in 'grunting and covered in mud and
eating raw hedgehog'. Anyway. During her fun days
in the woods she once took home a muddy frog in a
bucket, planning to clean it up nicely and keep it as
a pet. But her mum made her take it back. The frog
agreed with her mum.

Ali now lives in Southampton with her husband and
two teenage sons and a very small garden pond which
has never yet attracted any frogspawn or even half a
newt. Ali is trying not to take this personally.

Other books
in the **SWITCH** series

Spider Stampede

Fly Frenzy

Grasshopper Glitch

Ant Attack

Crane Fly Crash

Beetle Blast

SPECIAL DIARY ENTRY

SUBJECT: REPTOSWITCH FORMULA
ALMOST COMPLETE

Things are going well—very, very well actually. I've been working hard on the REPTOSWITCH formula and now it's (almost) perfect. Soon, I'll be able to SWITCH Danny and Josh into all kinds of scaly reptiles—lizards, chameleons, snakes, and even alligators! What a genius I am! No one else in the whole world knows how to change people into creatures—and now I can SWITCH people into insects and reptiles!

Anyway, before I can share my super genius-ness with the world, I need to test the formula a bit more. And I know just the two boys to help me. After all, who wouldn't want to find out what it's like to have the shell of a turtle, the forked-tongue of a snake, or the teeth of an alligator?

REMEMBER

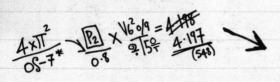

Maybe, I'll just forget to mention to Danny and Josh what happened in my earlier experiments—I wouldn't want to worry them— I mean, so what if my test subjects were not quite themselves afterwards. You'd think a rat would be pleased to have constantly changing fur like a chameleon but instead he looked rather annoyed.

Yes, the less Josh and Danny know, the better. But I'll keep notes in my diary after every experiment. Watch out world—Genius Scientist Petty Potts is about to take her REPTOSWITCH formula to the next level!

GET READY FOR THE NEXT SIX SWITCH BOOKS— COMING TO BOOKSHOPS SOON!

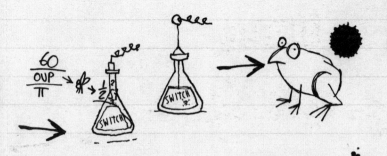

Whether you're curious about
crane flies or freaked out by frogs, you'll
love the SWITCH website.

Find out more about the creatures in
Josh and Danny's adventures, enter fantastic
competitions, read the first chapters
of all of the SWITCH books, and enjoy
creepy-crawly games and activities.

www.switch-books.co.uk